¿Qué tengo en el bolsillo, querido dragón?

What's in My Pocket, Dear Dragon?

por/by Margaret Hillert
ilustrado por/Illustrated by David Schimmell

NORWOOD HOUSE PRESS

Queridos padres y maestros:

La serie para lectores principiantes es una colección de lecturas cuidadosamente escritas, muchas de las cuales ustedes recordarán de su propia infancia. Cada libro comprende palabras de uso frecuente en español e inglés y, a través de la repetición, le ofrece al niño la oportunidad de practicarlas. Los detalles adicionales de las ilustraciones refuerzan la historia y le brindan la oportunidad de ayudar a su niño a desarrollar el lenguaje oral y la comprensión.

Primero, léale el cuento al niño; después deje que él lea las palabras con las que está familiarizado y pronto, podrá leer solito todo el cuento. En cada paso, elogie el esfuerzo del niño para que se sienta más confiado como lector independiente. Hable sobre las ilustraciones y anime al niño a relacionar el cuento con su propia vida.

Sobre todo, la parte más importante de la experiencia de la lectura es ¡divertirse y disfrutarla!

Shannon Cannon

Shannon Cannon
Consultora de lectoescritura

Norwood House Press • P.O. Box 316598 • Chicago, Illinois 60631
For more information about Norwood House Press please visit our website at *www.norwoodhousepress.com* or call 866-565-2900.
Text copyright ©2014 by Margaret Hillert. Illustrations and cover design copyright ©2014 by Norwood House Press, Inc. All rights reserved. No part of this book may be reproduced or utilized in any form or by any means without written permission from the publisher.
Designer: The Design Lab

LIBRARY OF CONGRESS CATALOGING-IN-PUBLICATION DATA
Hillert, Margaret.
  [What's in my pocket, dear dragon? Spanish]
  ¿Qué tengo en el bolsillo, querido dragón? = What's in my pocket, dear dragon? / por Margaret Hillert ; ilustrado por David Schimmell ; traducido por Queta Fernandez.
    pages cm. -- (A beginning-to-read book)
  Summary: "A boy and his pet dragon learn about sizes and colors as they put items in and take items out of different pockets. This title includes reading activities"-- Provided by publisher.
  ISBN 978-1-59953-611-8 (library edition : alk. paper) -- ISBN 978-1-60357-619-2 (ebook)
  [1. Pockets--Fiction. 2. Color--Fiction. 3. Size--Fiction. 4. Dragons--Fiction. 5. Spanish language materials--Bilingual.] I. Schimmell, David, illustrator. II. Fernandez, Queta, translator. III. Hillert, Margaret. ¿Qué tengo en el bolsillo, querido dragón? IV. Hillert, Margaret. What's in my pocket, dear dragon? Spanish. V. Title. VI. Title: What's in my pocket, dear dragon?
  PZ73.H5572075 2014
  [E]--dc23
               2013034963

Manufactured in the United States of America in Brainerd, Minnesota.
240N—012014

Tengo bolsillos, querido dragón.
Es bueno tener bolsillos.
Tú no tienes bolsillos.

I have pockets, Dear Dragon.
Pockets are good to have.
You do not have pockets.

3

Adivina qué hay en este bolsillo, querido dragón.
¿Puedes adivinar qué hay en mi bolsillo?

Guess what is in this pocket, Dear Dragon.
Can you guess what's in my pocket?

Te ayudaré.

Es una canica negra.

Yo juego con ella.

I'll help you.

It is a black marble.

I play a game with it.

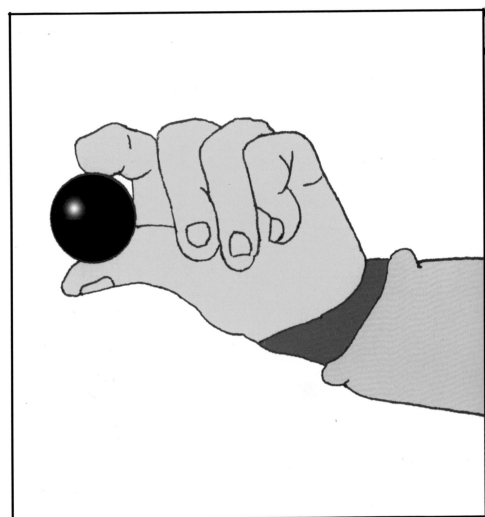

Mira aquí.   Here.
Te lo muestro.   I'll show you.

Y tengo esto.
Mira lo que puedo hacer con él.

And I have this.
See what I can do with it.

Oh, oh.
Ahí va.
Míralo como va.

Oh, oh.
There it goes.
Look at it go.

Aquí hay algo para comer.   Here is something to eat.
¿La quieres?   Do you want some?
Es buena.   It is good.

Tengo dos bolsillos.
¿Qué hay en este?
Adivina. Adivina.

I have two pockets.
What is in this one?
Guess. Guess.

Caramba.
Es un carrito azul.
Me gusta jugar con él,
pero hay que hacer esto primero.

Oh, my.
It is a blue car.
I like to play with it.
But, you have to do this first.

Avanza, carrito, avanza.
Corre para aquí. Corre para allá.

Go little car, go.
Run here. Run there.

Sube.

Run up.

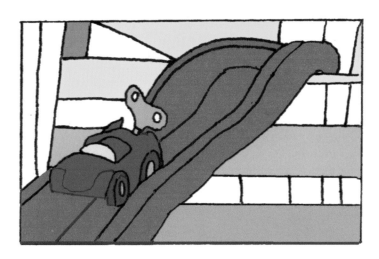

Baja.

Run down.

Oh, no. Ahora no puede avanzar.

Oh, no. Now it can not go.

Ahora, mira lo que tengo aquí.
Puedo hacer algo con esto.

Now, look what I have here.
I can make something with it.

Vamos a entrar a la casa.

Let's go into the house.

Ponlo aquí.

Put this here.

Mira esto. También estaba en mi bolsillo.
Lo guardaré aquí.

Look at this. This was in my pocket, too.
I'll put it away in here.

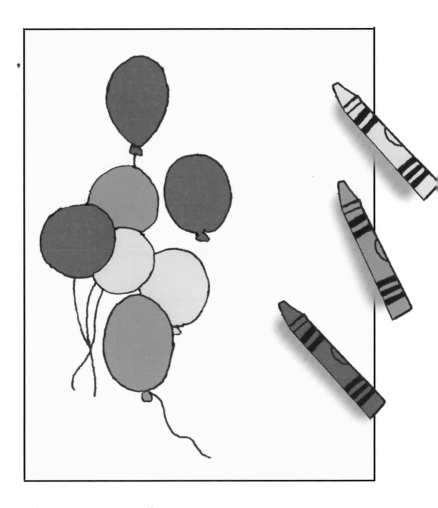

También tengo algunos crayones.
Uno es rojo. Otro es amarillo.
Otro es verde. Los crayones son divertidos.

I have some crayons, too.
One is red. One is yellow.
One is green. Crayons are fun.

Mamá, mamá.
¿Puedes hacerle un bolsillo a dragón?

Mother, Mother.
Can you make a pocket for Dragon?

Bueno, déjame pensar.
Creo que tengo algo.

Well, let me see.
I think I have something.

¿Servirá esto?
Dragón, ven a ver.
Parece un bolsillo grande.

Will this do?
Dragon, come see this.
It looks like a big pocket.

Es bueno.
Podemos poner cosas en él.

That is good.
We can put things in.

Podemos sacar cosas de él.

We can take things out.

Tú estás conmigo
y yo estoy contigo.
Somos buenos amigos, querido dragón.

Here you are with me.
And here I am with you.
We are good friends, Dear Dragon.

The following activities support the findings of the National Reading Panel that determined the most effective components for reading instruction are: Phonemic Awareness, Phonics, Vocabulary, Fluency, and Text Comprehension.

Phonemic Awareness: The /p/ sound

Oddity Task: Say the /**p**/ sound for your child. Say the following words aloud. Ask your child to say the words that do not end with the /**p**/ sound in the following word groups:

pat, tap, mat	park, map, pack	set, pet, step
peach, reach, sleep	met, pet, up	spot, top, ten
seat, pea, keep	mark, pop, speck	sheep, day, page

Phonics: The letter Pp

1. Demonstrate how to form the letters **P** and **p** for your child.

2. Have your child practice writing **P** and **p** at least three times each.

3. Ask your child to point to the words in the book that start with the letter **p**.

4. Write down the following words and ask your child to circle the letter **p** in each word:

play	help	pretty	puppy	pocket
jump	put	skip	nap	happy
peep	pan	pepper	stamp	purple

Vocabulary: Adjectives

1. Explain to your child that words that describe something are called adjectives.

2. Say the following nouns and ask your child to name an adjective that might be used to describe it (possible answers in parentheses):

car (fast)   flower (pretty)   apple (juicy)

marble (round)   coin (shiny)   sun (bright)

dog (soft)   crayon (little)   ice (cold)

3. Write the nouns on separate pieces of paper.

4. Randomly place the pieces of paper on a flat surface. Read each noun aloud to your child. Ask your child to point to the correct word.

5. Encourage your child to think of other adjectives that can describe each noun.

Fluency: Shared Reading

1. Reread the story to your child at least two more times while your child tracks the print by running a finger under the words as they are read. Ask your child to read the words he or she knows with you.

2. Reread the story taking turns, alternating readers between sentences or pages.

Text Comprehension: Discussion Time

1. Ask your child to retell the sequence of events in the story.

2. To check comprehension, ask your child the following questions:

- What objects does the boy take out of his pockets?
- What does the boy do with the balloon?
- What does Dear Dragon get for a pocket?
- What is in Dear Dragon's bag?
- What do you have in your pockets?

Margaret Hillert ha escrito más de 80 libros para niños que están aprendiendo a leer. Sus libros han sido traducidos a muchos idiomas y han sido leídos por más de un millón de niños de todo el mundo. De niña, Margaret empezó escribiendo poesía y más adelante siguió escribiendo para niños y adultos. Durante 34 años, fue maestra de primer grado. Ya se retiró, y ahora vive en Michigan donde le gusta escribir, dar paseos matinales y cuidar a sus tres gatos.

Photograph by Glenna Washburn

Margaret Hillert has written over 80 books for children who are just learning to read. Her books have been translated into many different languages and over a million children throughout the world have read her books. She first started writing poetry as a child and has continued to write for children and adults throughout her life. A first grade teacher for 34 years, Margaret is now retired from teaching and lives in Michigan where she likes to write, take walks in the morning, and care for her three cats.

David Schimmell fue bombero durante 23 años, al cabo de los cuales guardó las botas y el casco y se dedicó a trabajar como ilustrador. David ha creado las ilustraciones para la nueva serie de Querido dragón, así como para muchos otros libros. David nació y se crió en Evansville, Indiana, donde aún vive con su esposa, dos hijos, un nieto y dos nietas.

David Schimmell served as a professional firefighter for 23 years before hanging up his boots and helmet to devote himself to work as an illustrator. David has happily created the illustrations for the New Dear Dragon books as well as many other books throughout his career. Born and raised in Evansville, Indiana, he lives there today with his wife, two sons, a grandson and two granddaughters.